Hurricane
on the Way!

by Amy Copenhaver
illustrated by Gina Capaldi

Harcourt
SCHOOL PUBLISHERS

Printed in the United States of America

ISBN 10: 0-15-350520-6
ISBN 13: 978-0-15-350520-1

Ordering Options
ISBN 10: 0-15-350334-3 (Grade 4 Below-Level Collection)
ISBN 13: 978-0-15-350334-4 (Grade 4 Below-Level Collection)
ISBN 10: 0-15-357510-7 (package of 5)
ISBN 13: 978-0-15-357510-5 (package of 5)

1 2 3 4 5 6 7 8 9 10   179   12 11 10 09 08 07 06

The wooden ship sailed into the harbor. Thirteen-year-old William Franklin waited on the pier. A man climbed down the ladder to the dock.

"Captain Mason?" William said.

"Yes," the man replied.

"I am William Franklin. I am George Franklin's son," William said. "Have you brought everything? My father's order was for 50 pounds of tea and 100 pounds of coffee."

"It's all here," replied Mason. "Your father places the same order every year."

"We order a year's supply—no more and no less," William explained.

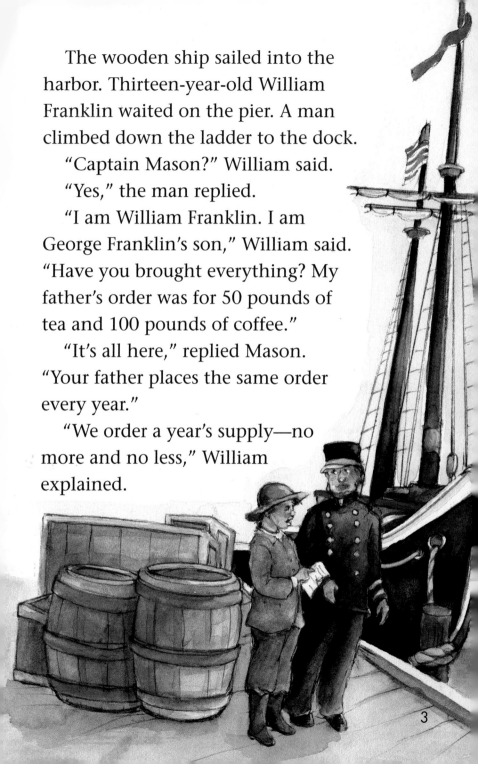

3

"Captain, may I help you unload?" William asked eagerly.

"Not today," Mason replied, rubbing his shoulder. "My shoulder tells me there's a big storm on the way, and my shoulder never lies. Look at the horizon, young man. Do you see those treacherous clouds building up? They mean a hurricane is on the way. If you want to help, hurry home and tell your family. You can pick up the coffee and tea after the storm."

Then Captain Mason told his first mate, "Spread the word to the other ships and to the townspeople. Everyone should prepare for the coming storm."

William hurried back to his family's farm. The quiet woods around him were a marked change from the noisy, busy port city.

Farm life was lots of drudgery and little play. Lately, however, George Franklin had begun to send his son on errands. William was proud that his father trusted him.

"Will, hurry and help," George Franklin called from the rice paddy when the boy had put away the horse and buggy. The farm workers plunged their hands into the watery field to tend the tall rice plants. They were the farm's most important crop.

"Father, what do shoulders have to do with storms?" William asked.

"Nothing," replied his father, skeptically.

"Captain Mason said that his shoulder tells him there is going to be a hurricane," William continued.

George Franklin's expression altered suddenly from amusement to concern. He looked hard at the sky.

"I know John Mason well," said William's father. "We worked on the docks together. A heavy crate fell on his shoulder once. That old injury acts up when a storm is on the way."

Will was telling his father about his trip
into town when his mother joined them.
"John's shoulder also hurt before the big storm
we had when you were a baby," she said. "I'll
never forget the waves and wind. Father was
stranded at the dock. The waves were so high,
and it rained so hard, that some of the houses
were underwater. I worried so until I got word
that Father was safe."

The fact that John Mason's shoulder was hurting was enough to make William's father take action. Everyone on the farm began to prepare for a hurricane. They tied down equipment, boarded up windows, and made sure the animals had food to last for a few days.

William's mother said to her son, "I am worried about Aunt Lydia. You know she is visiting Mrs. Carroll in town. The wind and waves will be stronger there. Please drive the wagon to Charleston and bring her back here."

William knew the situation was serious. However, he was secretly thrilled to drive back to town. Charleston was an exciting place.

As William drove through the streets, everyone was getting ready for the storm. The weather was still sunny, but it was unusually hot and humid. A steady breeze was blowing.

William neared Charleston Harbor. Usually, this was his favorite place to sit and watch the tall ships sail into port. There was no time to sit today. However, he decided to make a quick stop at Captain Mason's ship. Father would be pleased if Will brought the coffee and tea along with Aunt Lydia.

The crew was tired and discouraged from unloading so much heavy cargo so quickly. The entire harbor was filled with workers who were racing against time because of the coming hurricane. One of the crewmembers asked Will to please get out of his way.

When Captain Mason saw Will, he was smoldering with anger and yelled, "I told you to be on your way! We are trying to get everything unloaded before the hurricane arrives. I promise you that as soon as the hurricane passes you can come pick up your father's order."

William quickly climbed into the wagon and drove off. "No more stops," he promised himself. "I must get Aunt Lydia, and get home as soon as possible."

He arrived at a pretty wooden house, tied up the horses, and knocked. "I am here to fetch my Aunt Lydia," said William to Mrs. Carroll when she answered the door. "My mother is worried about Aunt Lydia getting through the hurricane safely."

Will discovered that leaving with Aunt Lydia was going to take more time than he had planned. First, he had to greet Mrs. Carroll's daughter who scoffed at the idea that Aunt Lydia should leave. "We have everything a person could need to get through a hurricane," said Mrs. Carroll's daughter.

"I see that you do," William said politely. "The only thing you do not have is distance from the water," William thought to himself. "Mother still remembers when father was caught in town during a storm," he continued aloud. "She doesn't want to feel that nervous again."

Finally, Aunt Lydia was safely in the wagon. William loaded her trunk in back, and they set off for the farm. They rode as fast as they could over the bumpy road. By this time, the sky was cloudy.

When William and Aunt Lydia pulled up to the farmhouse, his mother rushed to greet them. "I am so glad you are back safely!" she exclaimed.

Greetings were short, however. By now, a strong wind was blowing. As the first heavy drops of rain began to fall, the Williams family shut themselves safely inside their farmhouse to ride out the storm. Another hurricane was about to become a part of Charleston history.

Think Critically

1. How did William and his father know a hurricane was coming?

2. Why is it important that Captain Mason and George Franklin know each other personally?

3. What are some of William's good qualities?

4. What is another word that means almost the same thing as *drudgery* does on page 5?

5. Would you have wanted to live in Charleston at the time this story takes place? Why or why not?

 Science

Hurricane! Look in a book or on the Internet for information about hurricanes. You might find out where they happen and how they are formed. Write five facts about hurricanes.

School-Home Connection Talk with a family member or friend about what people should do to get ready when a big storm is coming.

Word Count: 1,005